Brenton & Johnny,
Happy Reading!
Katie F—

Portia Parrott and the Great Kitten Rescue
Book 1

Written by KATIE FRENCH

Illustrated by SHERRIÉ SAVAGE

Copyright

CONTENTS

Dedication

To Noelle and Miles
Portia lives because of you

CHAPTER 1

Chance of a Lifetime

My name is Portia Parrott. I am not a bird. Parrott is just my last name. I don't have a beak or clawed feet. But once I fit a whole sleeve of crackers in my mouth. Then I threw up.

I am seven. Daddy says I'm old enough to feed chicken guts to his alligators. But

only if he's with me.

My daddy is a herp-e-tologist. It means he touches snakes with his bare hands. He owns two alligator babies, two snakes, a skink with a blue tongue, and seven lizards.

Daddy says they're for research.

Mommy says that's why she doesn't live with him anymore.

This winter, Daddy has the chance of a lifetime! He's leaving his teaching job to go to Australia where people say "Ga'day, Mate" and "shrimp on the barbie." When he told me I couldn't go with him, I threw myself on the floor and had a baby temper tantrum. He just folded his arms and shook his head. So, I'm going to live with Mommy while he's gone.

Mommy moved to Florida six months ago when Bumpa, my grandpa got sick.

Florida is, like, a ba-gillion miles from our house in Michigan. Florida has gators and six types of venomous snakes. I tell Mommy this in the car on the way back from the airport. She tells me she is calling the exterminator.

When we get to Mommy's house, Amber, her house cleaner, opens the door.

"Portia!" she yells, hugging me too tight. "How are you?"

"Help!" I say into her shirt. "There's too much belly on me."

Mommy pulls me back. "Portia, be polite!" She tells me to be polite when she wants me not to tell the truth.

Amber makes mad eyebrows.

I pull my shirt up over my face to hide. Eastern Box Turtles can close their heads up in their shells. Some animals get all the luck.

"Come in, Portia." Amber leads me into the kitchen and points to a plate of chocolate chip cookies.

That's some kind of service they have here!

A ball of fur runs in, barking like crazy. I jump onto a kitchen chair. "A giant rat!"

Mommy runs in and picks the rat up! It wiggles like it wants to bite her. "He's not a rat. He's the new dog I was telling you about. This is Bartholomew. Bart for short."

Bart sounds like Barf. Its eyes are way too big. "Do you feed him to the gators?"

"No, silly. He's my dog."

Mommy lets the rat dog lick her face. I might not kiss Mommy until she washes. She sets him down. "Bart is nice."

But, Barf does not think I am nice. He

growls at my feet.

"He'll get used to you," Mommy says. She hands me a cookie.

"What's there to do around this joint?" I ask. The house looks pretty boring. Mommy has a lot of shelves with just one picture frame or one lonely sea shell. There must not be a flea market in Florida. In Michigan, Daddy and I go to the flea market all the time. You can get all the best stuff there like gold teeth and dancing hula girls.

"There's lots to do around here," Mommy says, looking at Amber.

Amber shrugs. "We have a park down the street."

"Any gators at the park?" I ask.

"I hope not," Mommy says.

"Darn."

"Portia, if you see an alligator I want

you to get away as fast as you can." She looks into my face very serious.

"Sure, sure," I say, but I secretly cross my toes. I want to see a Florida gator so bad!

Barf the dog starts barking his head off again, but this time it's at a cat in the backyard. I walk to the glass door and watch the cat jump onto Mommy's fence.

"Is that your cat?" I ask. Cookie crumbs fall on Barf's head. He'll thank me later.

Mommy stands beside me. "That's the neighbor's cat. Tiger's always jumping the fence to tease Bart." She opens the glass door and Barf tears out. The cat jumps into another yard.

"The fleabag must've had her kittens," Amber says.

"Kittens?" I ask.

Mommy shakes her head. "No kittens. Bart would have a field day."

I watch Barf bark and jump at the fence on his little doggie legs. It's kind of funny. My cookie is the real good kind with chocolate chips the size of eyeballs. Maybe Florida isn't so bad. But I still hope I get to see a gator real soon.

CHAPTER 2

Lizard Belly

After cookies, Mommy breaks the bad news. Tomorrow I have to go to school.

"I don't need school. All I need to know I learn from the Animal Planet. I know the difference between venomous and poisonous. A venomous snake would bite venom into someone. A poisonous frog would kill you if you licked it."

Mommy puts her hands on her hips. Amber takes the rest of the cookies away. Barf growls at my foot.

"I don't need to go to school," I say again. "Daddy says, 'Life is a school.'"

Mommy shakes her head. "Your daddy has his head in the clouds. You're going to school. Tomorrow."

Mommy takes my hand and walks me through her new house. It's a lot cleaner than Daddy's. There are no animals staring at you from cages. I bet there aren't any dead rat babies in her freezer either. There's a lot of flower pictures on the walls. And a picture of me as a baby. I have fat cheeks and a stupid ducky hat on.

"I look dumb as a baby," I say.

"You were so sweet as a baby." She walks me into a bedroom with a pink bedspread and an empty bookshelf and a treadmill. "This is your room."

I look at the flower wallpaper and squiggly curtains. "It could use some snakes."

Mommy frowns. "No snakes."

I point at the snake on my shirt. "This

is a re-tic-u-lating python. That means it's a squeezer. Daddy says I can have one for my next birthday. That's four months and six days away."

Mommy blows a breath out of her mouth. "I'll get your bag."

I sit on the bed and wait. This room feels lonely. No snakes. No lizards. If I at least had a lizard looking at me from his cage, my belly wouldn't feel all swirly.

Mommy says Daddy will try to call today, but the time zone is different in Australia. That means he's asleep when I'm awake. I'll stay awake all night to talk to Daddy. I need to know if the flying foxes there are really as big as Bernie, our neighbor's dog.

But Daddy doesn't call and Mommy makes me go to bed at 8:30 even when I say I'm not tired. Even when I say my brain is on Australia time. Even when I say the words "didgeridoo" and "dingo" to prove it.

The next morning, Mommy wakes me up with the sun. Daddy calls this ungodly early. It's when even God is asleep.

"Up and at 'em," she says.

I rub my fists into my eyeballs. "It's too early. I need a cup of coffee pronto."

She snorts. "Your father lets you drink coffee?"

"A non-fat caramel mocha, please." I push my floppy hair out of my eyes.

"How about cereal?"

When I get to the kitchen table, Mommy plops down a bowl of Raisin Bran.

"Daddy buys Lucky Charms," I say. The raisins look like bunny poops.

Mommy rolls her eyes and turns on the news.

Barf whines under the table. I guess he's done growling at my legs. I try to eat the bunny poop cereal, but my stomach is jumpy. When Mommy leaves the kitchen, I give the bowl to Barf. He licks the bowl clean. Maybe he isn't a stupid rat-dog.

All the way to school in Mommy's too-clean car, my stomach jumps and skips. It feels like a lizard lives in there. And lizards DO NOT like bunny poop cereal for breakfast.

When we get to the school, I pretend to be a chameleon. They can change colors. When Mommy opens my door, I sit perfectly still. This is called blending in. "Come on, Portia," she says, tapping her toe.

I don't move. "Can you see me?"

She sighs. "Of course."

"How much do I look like a seat?"

She frowns. "Come on. School's going to be fun."

But I'm pretty sure she's being polite. Which means she's lying.

CHAPTER 3

School of Doom

The school looks too big. And the kids are even bigger. Do they have, like, teenagers going here? The brick is crumbly and there aren't any palm trees. Daddy promised me palm trees. All I've seen is a few yellow, droopy ones down Mommy's street.

Mobs of children push past us. Mobs means they're probably going to mug us. I hold tight to my new backpack.

Mommy tugs me into the crowd. My skin prickles where the kids brush into me.

We start at the principal's office, which I know is a bad omen. And I know about omens 'cause one time Daddy let me watch three whole Indiana Jones movies. And they ate monkey brains! I know because when Daddy told me to cover my eyes. I did, but then I peeked between my fingers. And didn't sleep in my bed for a week.

The principal, Mrs. Herbert, smiles at me while Mommy explains about "home schooling." Home schooling is when your dad teaches you stuff from his herp-e-tol-ogy books and you get to stay in your pajamas and feed dead rat babies to the snakes. Sometimes we would go to the library. Sometimes we would watch cartoons.

A teacher comes in, takes me to a cold room with no pictures, and makes me take a test that hurts my head.

"My brain's still on Australia time," I say.

"Mmm hmm." The teacher smiles at me.

"Chameleons' eyes can look in two directions at once," I say.

She taps the test. "Just answer the questions, hun."

But I can't answer their dumb questions. They don't even ask about reptiles. The teacher lady brings me back and sits me in a chair and Mommy and the principal whisper.

The principal leans across her desk and smiles. I see at least three nose hairs in each nostril. It's like a forest in there. "How about first grade, Portia? Some of the students in first grade are seven like you."

I shrug. She blows out and her nose hairs dance.

The grown-ups stand and shake hands. Mommy steers me toward the door. The teacher lady who gave me the brain-squeezing test waits for us in the hallway.

"This way," she says, smiling. Grown-ups are always smiling at kids as they lead them to their doom on TV.

We pass classrooms with kids sitting in desks. "Daddy says learning should be fun," I say.

Mommy sighs.

The teacher lady stops at a room at the end of the hallway with puke green carpet. Mommy pushes me toward the door. I grab the frame and cling like a gecko. "Let's not go in, okay? I think if we hurry home we can watch Judge Judy." I look up, hopeful.

Inside, the teacher stops talking. Everyone stares at me. Mommy pushes harder. I cling on like a bird is trying to swoop down and eat me.

"Mrs. Corner, this is Portia," the teacher lady says. She starts helping Mommy pull me.

"Oh." Mrs. Corner's eyes get real big when she sees my gecko grip, 'cause it's powerful.

Mommy and the teacher lady pop me off the door. Mommy drags me to an empty chair, but I crawl under a table and curl up.

A boy wearing a Batman mask looks under the table at me. "Are you crazy?"

I stare at his Batman mask. "Are you?"

Mommy drags me out and plops me in the chair. I almost say, Daddy says life is a school, but her eyes are really big. Like bug's eyes. Like real mad bug eyes.

Mommy leaves, saying something about an aspirin. I practice blending in.

It works 'cause hardly anyone notices me. Except that Batman boy who thinks I'm crazy. He stares at me like I've got a bug on my head. But HE'S the one in a costume and it's not even Halloween. I make bug eyes at him.

He leans back. "You ARE crazy."

I smile. Daddy says crazy is what people say when they mean genius.

CHAPTER 4

You Need Spit

Batman boy's name is Mason. The other girl at our table, with black hair down to her bottom, is Veronica. I don't learn any of the other kids' names. I don't learn anything 'cause all Mrs. Corner talks about is adding. She puts a paper in front of me with all those brain-squeezing math problems. Batman boy and Veronica start numbers. I draw a python squeezing 2 + 4. Those numbers will be lunchmeat by the time my snake's done with them.

Mason looks at my python drawing. "Mrs. Corner won't be a happy camper."

I look squinty at him and draw a snake eating 3 + 2. His eyes go even bigger.

"Don't do that. You'll get sent to a loonie bin!"

I point at his mask. "Why are you wearing a mask? You aren't really Batman."

"I know." He pushes the mask off, which turns out to be extra fabric connected to the hood of his sweatshirt.

"Do you want to be Batman?" I ask.

"Yes! Do you want to be a snake?" he asks.

"Sometimes." I point to the one on my shirt. "Garter snakes eat toads."

He leans away. "You want to eat toads?"

"No." I cross my arms over my chest.

"What's wrong with your hair?"

I feel up my head. "What?"

"It's so… poofy," he says, pointing with his pencil.

I frown. "Mommy says I have my dad's wild hair." I pat the two poof balls

27

on each side of my head.

He looks at my hair for a while. "You need spit. That's what my mom does." He taps his shiny hair.

Mrs. Corner comes up behind us. "This is not talking time. This is working time. Mason, please get to work."

Mason drops his eyes and writes numbers.

Mrs. Corner looks at me. "How are we getting along?"

I shrug.

She looks at my paper. "Oh."

"Oh" is what grown-ups say when they are NOT impressed. I scribble over my snakes.

Mrs. Corner clears her throat. "Portia, will you follow me to the hall?"

I look at her face, and it seems nice, so I don't do my gecko grip on my chair.

When we get to the hall, she puts her hand on my shoulder. "It's okay if you don't know how to do the work right away. I don't want you to feel bad. We'll get you caught up."

I look at the ground.

"Did you and your dad work on numbers at all?"

I stare at my shoes. "I know how many poisonous lizards there are."

"Did he ever teach you to count or add single digits?" she asks.

"Sometimes." My eyes feel watery and my stomach is jumping again.

She pats me. "It's okay, Portia. You'll catch up in a hurry."

Mrs. Corner leads me back in. She's nice and I like her red high heels and her mushroom haircut, but I still wish I was in Australia.

CHAPTER 5

The Great Kitten Rescue

Amber picks me up after school. Before she drives away, she hands me a chocolate chip cookie. I like Amber.

"How was school?"

"Boring," I say through cookie bites.

"Did you make any friends?"

I shake my head. "There's a boy who thinks he's Batman. Everyone else is a stick in the mud."

Amber raises her eyebrows and looks at me in the rearview mirror. "Don't you think you should give them another chance?"

"Do you think you could roll down a window? My throat is dying." I paw at the car's window.

Amber shakes her head. "The air conditioning's on."

I make gagging noises and fake faint until she rolls down my window. It doesn't help. Florida air is hot like a dog's breath.

When we get home, Amber gives me another cookie. Barf, the rat-dog, forgets we are friends and growls at my foot again. I think he has a pee brain.

"Take Bart out in the yard and play

with him," Amber says as she wipes up cookie crumbs.

"It's as hot as a butt out there," I say. "Come on, Barf."

Barf runs to the door and whines until I open it. He runs out and dives on a drooly bone in the grass. I pick up the bone and it's drippy and oozy. It reminds me of chicken guts.

"Fetch!" I throw the bone. It falls in the bushes. Barf dives after it.

I sit down in the hot-breath Florida air and sweat. In Florida you sweat a lot. Even on Christmas.

Something plops next to my knee. A giant grasshopper! He's green and gold and the size of the rat babies we feed snakes. Daddy's python would go ga-ga. He's amazing! Michigan grasshoppers are grass-green and tiny and boring. I creep up on the big fella, trying to catch him, but he sproings away.

"Shoot!"

Barf runs back with something in his mouth. It's not the drooly bone. It has fur.

"Drop it, Barf!" I point my I-mean-it finger. He drops it.

The ball of fur is drippy and wadded up. I lean down and inspect it.

A kitten! He's brown and fuzzy, with little closed eyes and little ears and a big old tail. He doesn't look like a Michigan kitten, but if Florida grasshoppers can be huge, kittens might be weird, too. And he's all crumpled up.

"Bad Barf!" I say. Barf looks embarrassed. I guess it must be hard to be a dog and to want to chew on cute things all the time. I pick up the poor, drooly kitten and carry him into the house.

Inside, Amber is cleaning. If Amber sees the kitten, she'll make me take him outside. And Barf might chew on him some more. I have to save him! I put the kitten in my shirt and go to my room.

I find a shoebox in the closet and toss out the shoes. One of Mommy's shirts becomes his bed. I tuck him in. He looks better, but he's still sleeping. I guess getting chewed on takes a toll.

When I hear Mommy come home from work, I tuck the kitten under my bed. Daddy would understand, but Mommy won't. Kitten Pants will be my little secret. And secrets are okay as long as kittens are involved.

CHAPTER 6

Kitten Pants

In the morning, Kitten Pants is still sleeping. I poke him a little. Poor Kitten Pants. That Barf really is a trouble maker. I wonder if Mommy knows he's a kitten chomper.

"Time for school," Mommy yells.

I look at Kitten Pants. He can't be left alone. Barf would have a holiday chewing him up. I put the lid on the shoebox and

put the box in my backpack. Then I zip it up and put the backpack on.

Mommy opens my door and comes in my room. "All ready for school?"

I smile, but the lizards are jumping in my belly again. Maybe a secret from

Mommy isn't a good idea.

Barf runs in and starts sniffing my backpack. I shoo him away with my foot. "Stop, Barf!"

Mommy picks him up. "He must smell your dad's animals." She kisses Barf. He licks her face.

I hold my backpack tighter. How can Mommy kiss a kitten chewer?

"Ready?" she asks.

"Fine. Let's go, toots," I say.

The whole drive to school I'm sweaty and jumpy. I want to check on Kitten Pants, but Mommy would see. I hug my backpack and count palm trees. Four yellow trees. It's the Florida dog-breath air that's killing them, I tell you.

When I get to class, Mrs. Corner is passing out art supplies. I walk real careful to my chair and slip my backpack under my table.

"Backpacks go in your locker," Batman Mason says. But this time he isn't wearing his Batman mask. He has on another hooded sweatshirt with another mask-hood that he can pull over his eyes.

"Who are you today?" I ask.

"Captain America." He puts his hands on his hips. Tries to look beefed up.

"And what does Captain American do?" I look at my backpack. Is it moving?

"You don't know what Captain America does? Are you even from here?" He looks at me like I'm crazy again.

"No." This time I really think my backpack moves.

Mrs. Corner stands behind me. "Portia, your backpack goes in your locker. Here. Give it to me."

"I told her," Mason says, pushing back

his mask-hood.

I grab my backpack. "I'll just…keep it here." My jumpy stomach gets even jumpier.

"Let me hang it up for you." She grabs my backpack.

I grab my backpack, too. "I wanna keep it. For posterity."

Something wiggles inside. Mrs. Corner lifts up her eyebrows. "What the—"

"Please give it back!"

I yank the bag down. We both tug at the same time. The zipper lets go. The backpack pops open!

And out jumps Kitten Pants! Right onto Mrs. Corner's mushroom haircut!

CHAPTER 7

Disaster

Ah!" screams Mrs. Corner. "Oh no!" I yell.

Kitten Pants runs around like a maniac. He crawls into Mrs. Corner's shirt.

"Ah ah!" screams Mrs. Corner. She dances and jumps and tugs at her shirt. A bulge moves around. Kitten Pants is run-

ning all over inside that shirt! He is one hyper cat.

The other kids run over. Mason pulls his Captain America hood over his eyes. I hope Captain America's super power is stopping insane kittens.

Mrs. Corner runs around the room, swatting her body. She shakes her shirt open like my dad airing out his dirty underwear. She is in a panic! She makes noises like the turtle I saw giving birth on the inner net. Finally, Kitten Pants falls out. I run over to grab him, but he's a Speedy Gonzales. He darts across the carpet and into the bathroom. I run after him and close the bathroom door.

Inside the bathroom, he scampers around the tile from corner to corner. I might puke from all the excitement. Like that time on the tilt-a-whirl at the carnival. Blue Icee is still blue when it comes back up, in case you were wondering.

"Come here, Kitten Pants," I say sweetly. I make a curvy finger and coax him. Kitten Pants skitters around the floor and knocks over the trash can.

The door opens. Mrs. Corner looks in. Her hair looks like Daddy's when he first wakes up.

"Portia, come out," she pants. "You could get rabies."

"He's just a kitten," I say.

She shakes her head. "That," she points, "is a squirrel."

That is when I realize I need to give Kitten Pants a new name.

CHAPTER 8

Captain America to the Rescue

"Please come out, Portia. We'll call the janitor." She waves me to her, but doesn't come in.

"I have to get Kitten Pants," I say. "He got chewed on and now he's in a foreign land with no family and he's scared and it's all my fault." Now instead of puking, I feel like cry-babying. I rub my eyes. "He's all alone."

Mrs. Corner inches into the bathroom. She puts a hand on my shoulder. "But he isn't alone. He has you. Sometimes all you need is one really good person to care about you." She smiles and hugs me. She smells like lemon dishwasher soap.

Kitten Pants makes a mad break for it and Mrs. Corner screams and hides behind me.

There's a splash. Kitten Pants has leaped into the toilet and is splashing around in that joint. He does NOT look happy. "He's stuck in the toilet!" I yell.

"Oh no!" Mrs. Corner says. "We have to get him out!" She pushes open the bathroom door. "Class, I need something to grab the squirrel. Quick!"

Veronica runs over with a toy dinosaur. A girl with a spangley headband brings a tub of paste. Kitten Pants is

splashing up a storm and I'm worried. A guy could drown in there. Then he'd really have a pee brain.

Mason walks over. He takes off his Captain America sweatshirt, looks at it for a sad minute, and hands it to Mrs. Corner.

Mrs. Corner looks at Mason. "Are you

sure?"

Mason sighs. "To protect and serve. It is my duty."

Mrs. Corner rumples his hair.

She walks into the bathroom. All the kids squeeze in behind her to watch.

"If this things bites me, I better get a month's paid leave." She puts the sweatshirt on her hands and reaches into the toilet. A big splash of water slops out. Mrs. Corner yelps. Kitten Pants makes a weird chip chip noise. I bite my fingernails.

Mrs. Corner turns around. A very wet squirrel struggles in her hands. "Get the box!"

Some kids run to my backpack and get the shoebox. Mrs. Corner drops Kitten Pants in and shuts the lid. Then she tapes it closed with, like, a hundred rolls of tape. The shoebox jumps and hops, but

Kitten Pants is safe.

"You did it, Mrs. Corner!" Mason says.

All the children cheer!

Mrs. Corner smiles and pats Mason on the head. Then she goes to her desk and puts her head in her hands for a long time.

Mason walks over to me. "That was the most exciting thing that ever happened here!"

"Thanks for giving up your sweatshirt." I pat him.

He looks at the drippy thing on the bathroom floor. "It's okay. My mom can wash it. She loves laundry."

Mason and I sit down and watch Kitten Pants jump the shoebox around. "I need a new name," I say. "I can't call a squirrel Kitten Pants."

Mason thinks hard. "Is it a boy or a girl?"

"Boy. I think. I'm pretty sure."

Mason thinks some more. "How about Mr. Convincible? That's pretty much the best super hero name I can think of."

I nod and pat Mason on the back. "I couldn't have thunked of a better name myself."

I smile and look out the window. And guess what I see. A palm tree! An honest to goodness alive palm tree. And that's when I decide today is the best day ever!

Until the principal comes in.

CHAPTER 9

Toilet Squirrel

The principal takes a look around our room and makes an oh-my-goodness face. Mrs. Corner lifts her head from her desk. "It's a long story."

The principal turns toward me. "Portia, I need to see you in my office."

"Uh oh," Mason says.

If my stomach had lizards before, now it has giant eels swirling around. I look up at Principal Herbert. She looks mad as a cobra.

"This way," she says. Her face gets more wrinkles on it. Maybe I could tell her about Mommy's magic wrinkle cream behind the bathroom mirror, but I figure it's best to keep my lips zipped. At least where principals are concerned.

We walk down the hall. I count my breaths until my doom. I hope Mason will take care of Mr. Convincible when I'm in school jail.

Principal Herbert leads me in her office and shuts the door. She points to a chair. "Portia, I—"

"I didn't mean to make the squirrel go in the toilet! I couldn't keep him at home or Barf would have chomped him. And

Mrs. Corner was a hero. Don't get mad at her because she got toilet water on the carpet. It's my fault." I drop my head to her desk with a thunk.

Principal Herbert says nothing. When I look up, her eyes are glued to me. "What are you talking about?"

"Mrs. Corner didn't call you?"

She shakes her head slowly. "What squirrel? What toilet?"

"Um, never mind." I try a smile.

She frowns. "We'll get to that later. I called you down because your father is on the phone."

"What?" I throw my arms out and knock over a picture of Principal Herbert's family. "My dad is on WHAT phone?"

"This one," she says, handing it to me.

I press the phone to my ear. "Daddy?"

"Portia, honey! How are you?" Daddy

says through the phone. "How are things in Florida?"

"How are things in Australia? Are the flying foxes as big as Bernie?"

"Yes," Daddy says. "And you should see the snakes!"

"Are they huge?"

"Of course!" Daddy says. "As big as you. Bigger!"

"How's being on TV?"

"I'm not on TV yet," he says. "We're

just setting up. I miss you."

"I miss you too, Daddy." Cry-baby tears squirt out of my eyeballs. I lower my head so the principal can't see. "I wish you'd come home."

"But is Florida working out?" he asks.

I don't answer right away. I think of Mommy and Amber and Barf. I think of chocolate chip cookies and palm trees and squirrels. I think of Mason giving up his sweatshirt and Mrs. Corner saving the day.

"Yeah, I guess. Will you bring me back a python? A ginormous one?"

Daddy laughs. "Sure, baby girl. Gotta go."

I smile when I hang up the phone.

The principal smiles, too. Then her face gets that serious-business-mister look. "Let's talk about that toilet squirrel."

CHAPTER 10

Catch and Release

"I love you, Portia, but you cannot keep the squirrel. He might have rabies." Mommy looks at the jumping shoebox on our kitchen table.

"Why does everyone keep saying that? He isn't floaming at the mouth."

"Foaming," Mommy says. "And he

hasn't sat still long enough for us to tell."

I press my eye to one of the tiny holes we punched in the shoebox lid. Mr. Convincible throws his body up and nearly knocks my head off. He IS pretty insane. "I could train him."

Mommy shakes her head. "Why didn't you tell me you found a squirrel? We don't keep secrets in this family, young lady."

I look at my knees. "I didn't want you to take him away. I've never owned a kitten before. Or a squirrel."

She sighs and taps on the box. "You can't always have what you want, Portia. Honesty is more important than a squirrel."

I nod. "I liked him better when he was sleeping anyway."

"We'll let him go outside."

I shake my head. "What about—"

"We'll keep Bart inside until Mr. Convincible has scampered away."

I hug the box, but Mr. Convincible is still trying to knock my head off from inside. "Okay. Let's take care of this business."

Mommy walks with me out the backdoor and locks Barf inside. He claws at the glass. He'd give anything to chomp a kitten or a squirrel again. We set the box on the grass. Mommy holds up scissors to cut the tape. I press my mouth close to the breathy holes. "Goodbye, Mr. Convincible. You were the best pet I ever had in Florida. I'll never forget you…unless I get a snake." I flick my eyes over at Mommy, and she shakes her head. "Anyway, stay away from Barf and other dogs who want to chomp you. And come and visit me."

It's kinda sad, but I don't cry because I'm seven. And because this squirrel is insane.

Mommy cuts the tape. The lid flies off and Mr. Convincible jumps out of the box. He scampers over the lawn and up the fence. He sits up there for a while and chips at us like we're the most annoying people in the world.

Mommy takes my shoulder. "Come inside before that thing decides to come

back for revenge."

When we get in, Amber is just getting back from the store. She has a big glass box in her arms. An aquarium! I almost knock her down running to see. Inside are two tiny green lizards!

"Are these for me?" I jump and jump. The lizards hide under a fake log. And they have a fake tiki hut. I've always wanted a fake tiki hut!

Amber smiles and sets the aquarium on the counter. "They're lizards called anoles. The guy at the pet store said they were easy to take care of." Amber looks at Mommy. Mommy makes mad eyes at Amber. "They were on sale?" she says to Mommy.

"I love them! I love them! This one is Vince like Daddy's lizard. And this one is Taily 'cause of his long tail. Can I keep them in my room? Please, please!"

Amber looks at Mommy. Mommy throws up her hands. "Fine. Fine. But if you try to take them to school in a shoebox, they're Bart's breakfast. Got me?"

I squeal and grab the aquarium and almost drop it. Amber picks it up for me and carries it to my room. Mommy says something about needing a vacation.

Amber sets the aquarium on an empty shelf. She plugs in the heating pad and talks to me about feeding them. I nod even though I'm an expert at feeding lizards already.

She says we'll tell Mommy about the mealworms in the fridge tomorrow.

Portia Parrott Book 2 is coming soon!
To find out when, visit my website
www.katiefrenchbooks.com to learn more.

Made in the USA
Lexington, KY
01 March 2018